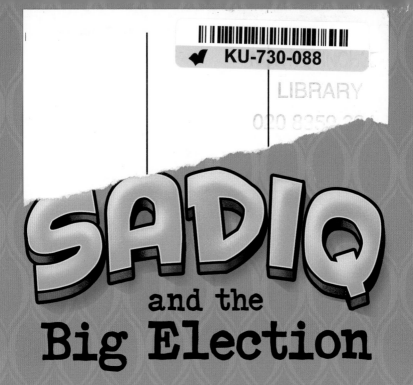

SADIQ

and the
Big Election

BY SIMAN NUURALI

ART BY CHRISTOS SKALTSAS

Raintree is an imprint of Capstone Global Library Limited, a company
incorporated in England and Wales having its registered office at
264 Banbury Road, Oxford, OX2 7DY – Registered company number:
6695582

www.raintree.co.uk
myorders@raintree.co.uk

Design by Tracy Davies
Design Element: Shutterstock/Irtsya
Original illustrations by Anjan Sarkar
Original illustrations © Capstone Global Library Limited 2022
Originated by Capstone Global Library Ltd
Printed and bound in India

ISBN 978 1 3982 3547 2

British Library Cataloguing in Publication Data
A full catalogue record for this book is available from the British Library.

CONTENTS

FACTS ABOUT SOMALIA

- Somali people come from many different clans.
- Many Somalis are nomadic. That means they travel from place to place. They search for water, food and land for their animals.
- Somalia is mostly desert. It doesn't rain often there.
- The camel is an important animal to Somali people. Camels can survive a long time without food or water.
- Around ninety-nine per cent of all Somalis are Muslim.

SOMALI TERMS

baba (BAH-baah) a common word for father

hooyo (HOY-yoh) mother

qalbi (KUHL-bee) my heart

salaam (sa-LAHM) a short form of Arabic greeting, used by many Muslims It also means "peace".

wiilkeyga (wil-KAY-gaah) my son

CHAPTER 1

AN ANNOUNCEMENT

Sadiq walked into his classroom on Friday morning. Some kids were standing in groups talking about their plans for the weekend. Others were settling into their chairs when Ms Battersby came in.

"Okay, everyone, please sit down!" said Ms Battersby. "I have an exciting announcement. Do you know what elections are?"

Sadiq's friend Manny put his hand up.

"It's when you vote for someone
to do something," Manny said.

"Good answer, Manny!" said Ms Battersby.
"We vote for people to be leaders. Next week,
we will be having our own elections. Our
class will have a student council."

"That's awesome!" said Manny.

"Yes, Manny, it is," said Ms Battersby.
"Our student council will have four different
roles, including the president. Does anyone
know what the president does?"

"They run the world!" said Zaza.

"Not quite, Zaza," said Ms Battersby,
smiling.

Zaza shrugged and smiled back.

"A president is like a prime minister. Presidents and prime ministers lead governments in making rules to help people," Ms Battersby said. "The school council president makes rules for the class. We will have a treasurer who will keep track of money and a secretary who will help things run smoothly. A vice president will help the president lead."

"Student government sounds like a lot of work," said a shy girl named Suliat.

"Can we choose to be what we want?" asked Aadya.

"You can run for what you like, Aadya," Ms Battersby said. "But people have to vote for you. And Suliat's right. It can be a lot of work – and a lot of fun!"

"I want to be in charge so I can cancel school," said Owen, laughing.

"Nice try, Owen," said Ms Battersby, shaking her head. "That is not what government is for. You have to try and make things better. You can't use it to cancel things."

Ms Battersby explained how voting would work. The students could submit their names for the election next week.

The kids were still chatting excitedly as they took out their books for the science lesson.

***

"Salaam, Hooyo!" said Sadiq, walking in the door after school.

"Salaam, Sadiq," said Hooyo. "How was your day, qalbi?"

"It was great!" said Sadiq. "Ms Battersby said we will have elections for the student council. I am thinking about running."

"What do you want to run for?" asked Hooyo.

"I haven't decided," said Sadiq. "There are four places. President, vice president, treasurer and secretary."

"Well, those all sound great," said Hooyo. She finished writing a cheque and pointed to an envelope on the table. "Hand me that, please."

"What are you sending, Hooyo?" asked Sadiq.

"I am paying the electric bill," she replied. "These are our bills for the month. I send cheques to pay for them."

"Is it really hard to do?" asked Sadiq.

"It can be if I don't budget well," said Hooyo.

"What does it mean to budget?" asked Sadiq.

"I calculate all our bills for the month," said Hooyo. She placed the cheque in the envelope.

"I make sure we have enough money to pay them. I also try to save a little every month. That's why your baba and I go to work. We use the money we earn to look after our family." Hooyo smiled at Sadiq.

"Budgeting sounds like a hard job," said Sadiq. "Is that what a treasurer does?"

"Yes, it is, qalbi," said Hooyo. "Is that what you want to run for?"

"I was thinking about it," said Sadiq, tilting his head. "But now I am not so sure. I like maths. But I'm not interested in budgets."

"Well, that's okay," said Hooyo. "You can run for one of the other positions."

"I'll think about it," said Sadiq. "Thanks, Hooyo."

Sadiq went upstairs to talk to his sister, Aliya. Maybe she would have some advice. When he got to her room, she was watching a video on her tablet.

"What are you watching?" he asked.

"It's for my history class," replied
Aliya. "I have to take notes and write a
report."

Sadiq flopped on his sister's bed. He
liked Aliya's room. The green walls
reminded him of the football pitch.

Aliya stopped working. "What's going on with you?" she asked.

"I want to run for the student council," he said. "I thought about being the treasurer. But now I'm not sure."

"How about secretary?" asked Aliya. "You could take notes for all the meetings."

"Is that what a secretary does?" asked Sadiq, frowning.

Aliya nodded. "It helps to keep a record of decisions the group makes. I like taking notes for my homework. It helps me remember what I'm learning."

"I don't want to take notes all the time. My hand would get tired!" said Sadiq. "I don't think I want to be the secretary."

"You will run out of positions soon," said Aliya, grinning.

"I have two more I can think about," said Sadiq. He threw a pillow at his sister.

"Sadiq!" shouted Aliya, laughing.

Sadiq went to the room he shared with his brother, Nuurali. He turned on the computer to do some research. Sadiq wanted to learn about presidents.

Sadiq learned that presidents listen to what people need. He learned that presidents sign laws. He learned that presidents try to make things better for everyone. That sounded great to Sadiq!

"I think I want to run for president," he whispered to himself.

CHAPTER 2

SADIQ MAKES A DECISION

It was a bright, sunny morning as Sadiq walked to school. He saw Zaza ahead of him and ran to catch up. Soon Manny joined them too.

"I am really excited about the student council," said Sadiq. "I wonder who's going to run for it."

"I think it would be a lot of fun," said Zaza. "Are you guys going to run?"

"Well, I –" Sadiq started.

"I'm running for president!" interrupted Manny. "I think I would make a really good one."

Sadiq was surprised – and worried. Could he run against Manny? Would they still be friends? Maybe he shouldn't run for president after all.

"I talked to my baba, and he thinks I would be great!" Manny continued.

"Were you going to say something, Sadiq?" asked Zaza.

"No," said Sadiq, shaking his head.

The boys went into the classroom and sat down.

"I think I'll run for secretary," said Owen. "I like taking notes. I could also organize the meetings."

"How about you, Suliat?" asked Zaza. "Will you run for anything?"

"I want to be treasurer," said Suliat. "I like maths, and my mum says I am good at saving money."

Sadiq quietly took out his books.

***

"Salaam, Baba," said Sadiq, walking into the living room.

"Salaam, wiilkeyga," replied Baba. "Are you okay? You don't look happy."

"I am okay, Baba," said Sadiq, sitting next to his dad. "I wanted to run for president, but I can't now."

"Oh? Why not?" asked Baba.

"Manny said he wanted to run," said Sadiq. "He said it before me."

"But wiilkeyga, more than one person can run," said Baba. "It's great if Manny wants to run, but so can you."

"I know," said Sadiq. "But I don't want to run against Manny. He might get cross with me and stop being my friend. That would make me really sad."

Sadiq looked down at his feet. He didn't know what to do.

"Tell me why *you* want to run," Baba said. "What are some of your ideas?"

"Sometimes break time isn't fair," said Sadiq. "Some kids don't get a turn on the climbing wall. Some of the bigger kids take extra turns."

"What would you do about that?" asked Baba.

"I would make rules about taking turns," replied Sadiq. "Everyone gets to go at least once. If there is time left, they can go a second time."

"That's really nice of you to think of everyone," said Baba. "What else would you like to do?"

"I've written a list, Baba," said Sadiq. "Would you like to see it?"

"Of course," said Baba. Sadiq reached into his backpack. He brought out a notebook and opened it.

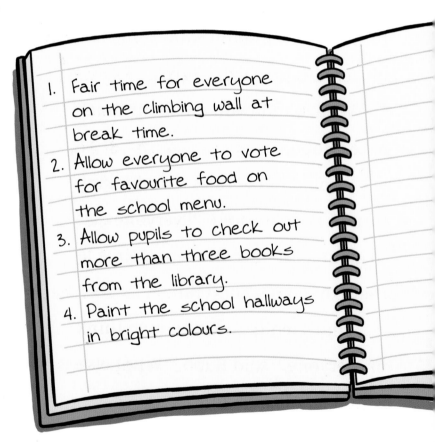

1. Fair time for everyone on the climbing wall at break time.
2. Allow everyone to vote for favourite food on the school menu.
3. Allow pupils to check out more than three books from the library.
4. Paint the school hallways in bright colours.

"These are great ideas, Sadiq," Baba said. "Did you think of them yourself?"

"Yes, I did!" replied Sadiq. "But it doesn't matter now. I will never be president."

"You can try," Baba replied. "I know it's scary to compete with a friend. But if you believe in your ideas, you have to. That's how you follow your dreams."

"I think I could help people, Baba," said Sadiq. "It's my dream to make things better for my class at school."

"You never have to give up just because it's scary," said Baba. He rubbed the top of Sadiq's head. "I get scared sometimes too, but I don't let that stop me from doing important things."

"You get scared?" Sadiq could not imagine that!

"Of course!" said Baba. "Everyone does."

"Thank you, Baba," said Sadiq. "I think I will run for president. I hope Manny doesn't get cross with me."

"Well, he might," said Baba. "But he will get over it. Your friendship is strong."

CHAPTER 3

A FRIENDLY COMPETITION

The next morning, Sadiq met Zaza
and Manny in the playground. They
had a few minutes before they had to go
into class.

"Are you guys going to sign up for the
student council today?" Zaza asked.

"I am," said Manny. "I can't wait
to run for president. How about you,
Zaza?"

"Oh, I am not running," said Zaza, smiling. "I thought it would be more fun to vote for my friends."

"Well, you can vote for me for president!" said Manny, puffing up his chest.

"How about you, Sadiq?" asked Zaza.

"Well, I . . . ," started Sadiq as he kicked the kerb.

"Maybe you can be my vice president," said Manny. He gave his friend a big smile.

"Come on, Sadiq, tell us!" said Zaza. "Will you be Manny's vice president?"

Sadiq hesitated. He didn't want to upset Manny. But he knew he had to follow his dream, so he spoke up.

"I . . . wanted . . . to run for president too," he finally said.

Manny stopped walking. "You can't!" he said. "*I* am the one running for president."

"Sadiq can run too, Manny," said Zaza. "You both can. That's how elections work."

"Are you taking his side?" asked Manny. "Are you going to vote for him?"

"I don't know," said Zaza. "I need to think about it."

"Fine!" said Manny. "You can vote for him. I don't care anyway." He walked away.

"I think he's really angry," Sadiq said. "I was worried this might happen."

Sadiq and Zaza went into the classroom.

Ms Battersby had put up some rules about running for the student council. One of them said that candidates had to give a speech. That way the other students could hear their ideas. It would help them choose who to vote for.

The idea of speaking in front of the whole class made Sadiq very nervous!

"Here's the sign-up sheet," said Zaza.

"I am going to think about it," replied Sadiq. He wasn't so sure about running for president any more.

***

After school, Sadiq waited around.

He wanted to speak to Ms Battersby.

"What's up, Sadiq?" she asked.

"I've got a hard decision to make," he replied. "I want to run for president, but Manny is upset with me. He wants to be president too. I don't want to lose him as a friend."

"I don't think that will happen, Sadiq," said Ms Battersby. "I am sure he doesn't want to lose you as a friend, either. If you focus on your campaign, it will be okay."

"I am also scared to give a speech," Sadiq admitted. "Maybe running for president is too hard."

Sadiq was worried, but Ms Battersby smiled at him.

"It's nice you're thinking about your friend," she said. "And I know that speaking in front of the whole class can be scary. But doing hard things is how you grow and learn."

"So, you think I should run?" asked Sadiq.

"Elections are about ideas," Ms Battersby said. "You always have interesting ideas. I think the class would like to hear them."

"Thank you, Ms Battersby," said Sadiq. "I think I will give it a try!"

Sadiq wrote his name on the sign-up sheet. Then he picked up his backpack and walked out of class. Zaza was waiting for him.

"What did Ms Battersby say?" he said.

"She said Manny will be okay," replied Sadiq. "She also said I should think about my ideas. That's what elections are about. She thinks I should go for it."

"That's good advice, Sadiq," said Zaza. "So, what did you decide?"

"I decided to do it," said Sadiq. He smiled. "I'm running for president!"

"That's awesome!" said Zaza. "But now *I* have a problem. Who will I vote for? You're both my best friends."

"That's okay, Zaza," replied Sadiq, smiling. "I will work on my speech to convince you. You don't have to choose now."

"What are some of your ideas?" asked

Zaza. "Will you say that we can play video games in lessons?"

"Hahaha. No, Zaza, don't be silly," laughed Sadiq. "I want fairness at break time for the climbing wall."

"If you say yes to video games, then you can have my vote!" Zaza teased.

"You will have to listen to my speech," said Sadiq. "I think you'll like my other ideas too!"

The two friends chatted and laughed as they walked home.

CHAPTER 4

CAMPAIGN WEEK

Sadiq opened the door to his house
and took off his shoes.

"Salaam, Baba!" he called to his dad.

"Here comes the candidate!" said
Baba.

"How is it going, qalbi?" asked Hooyo.

"I don't know, Hooyo," said Sadiq as
he hugged his mum. "Manny is cross
with me. I have to give a speech. It's
A LOT."

"Help me set the table," said Aliya. She handed Sadiq a pile of plates. "You can tell us about it."

"I have to use my speech to get votes," said Sadiq. "I can talk about my ideas and why they're the best."

"Does everyone have to give a speech?" asked Nuurali.

"If you want to get votes, yes," replied Sadiq. "Ms Battersby says it's important. You can change people's minds."

"I think you'll do well," said Nuurali. "You are very convincing. We always end up watching your pick for movie night!"

Sadiq smiled. "I have good suggestions!"

"I can help you practise your speech," offered Aliya.

"And I'll help you with your posters," said Nuurali. "I've got some coloured card. And Aliya has some new felt-tips too."

"You guys are the best!" said Sadiq, grinning.

***

The next morning, Sadiq carried his campaign posters to school. He spotted Zaza and rushed to catch up with him.

"Hi, Zaza!" said Sadiq.

"Hey, Sadiq!" replied Zaza. "Are those your posters?"

"Yeah," said Sadiq. "Would you like to see them?"

Sadiq showed the posters to Zaza.

"These are brilliant, Sadiq!" said Zaza. "Did you make them yourself?"

"I did, but Nuurali helped a lot!" said Sadiq.

They saw Manny across the road. He was carrying his posters too.

"Hey, Manny!" shouted Zaza. "Can we see your posters?"

"Sorry," Manny replied. "I have to run, or I'll be late for school. See you later." He didn't even look at them.

"We still have thirty minutes!" Zaza called to Manny. But he had already hurried away.

"I think he's still angry," said Sadiq, sadly.

"I'll help you put your posters up," said Zaza. "Cheer up, Sadiq. It will be okay."

"I hope so," replied Sadiq. "I've tried to talk to him. But he always finds an excuse to walk away."

"Maybe he had stuff to do," said Zaza.

"But we always do stuff together," said Sadiq. "Now he won't talk to me."

"I think he's just focusing on the election," said Zaza. "I'm sure once it's over we'll all be friends again."

"I wish I could tell him it's not personal," said Sadiq. "I want to run for president because it's important to me. But our friendship is important too!"

***

It was the day before the election. Something was strange in the house when Sadiq got home from school. It was dark. His family was not there.

"Hello?" Sadiq called.

"Surprise!" his family shouted. They stepped out of their hiding places.

"What's happening?" asked Sadiq, eyes widening.

"We are making an election dinner!"
said Hooyo, smiling.

"We thought it would cheer you up,"
said Baba.

"We picked all your favourite foods," said Aliya. "I helped make the samosas."

"Thank you," said Sadiq. "That's just what I needed!"

"Sadiq for president!" piped up his little sister, Rania.

"High five for Sadiq," said Amina, his other little sister.

"High five!" said Sadiq, laughing.

"We think you'll do really well, Sadiq!" said Hooyo. "You have good ideas. And you have practised your speech all week."

"Even if you don't win, you tried your best," said Baba. "And that's all that matters!"

CHAPTER 5

ELECTION DAY!

Sadiq walked into class and sat next to Manny and Zaza. The students were chattering with excitement. It was election day!

"How do you guys feel?" asked Zaza. "Are you ready?"

"Actually, I'm nervous," Manny said. "I feel like I won't be able to talk."

"I think you'll do great, Manny!" said Sadiq. "Just remember to breathe, and you'll be okay!"

"Aren't you scared?" asked Manny.

"I really am!" said Sadiq. "My tummy feels squishy like jellyfish. My knees are shaking. And my throat feels as dry as sand."

"That makes me feel better," said Manny, smiling. "Thank you!"

Ms Battersby clapped her hands to get everyone's attention. It was time for the speeches.

"Sadiq Mohamed!" she called out. "Come up and address the class, please."

"Wish me luck!" Sadiq said to Manny.

"Good luck!" said Manny.

Sadiq saw all his friends staring at him. It felt like there were a hundred kids in the class!

"I think . . . I should be class president," started Sadiq. But he was so nervous he forgot his speech!

He took a deep breath, just like he told Manny to do. That helped. He saw his good friend Manny grinning up at him. That helped even more. It all came back to him.

"I would make break time fair," he said. "I would make sure everyone gets to go on the climbing wall who wants to. It's not fair for only a few people to get a chance. I would make new rules. And everyone would get equal time."

The students clapped at that. They liked this idea!

"I also think we should vote on the lunch menu," said Sadiq. "Everyone can pick their favourite food, and we'll ask the headteacher to add it to the menu."

"Yay, Sadiq!" someone yelled.

"Sadiq for president!" said someone else.

"Quiet, everyone," said Ms Battersby. "Let Sadiq finish his speech."

"We can only check out three books from the library," said Sadiq. "I would ask the librarian to change that to five. I know we all like to read. So everyone can get more books to take home!"

"That gets my vote!" Owen called out.

"Finally, I think the main hallway looks a bit dull, especially on cloudy days," said Sadiq. "We could form a club and paint it bright colours. Then it would be cheerful all the time!"

Sadiq paused.

"Anything else, Sadiq?" asked Ms Battersby.

"I hope you'll all vote for me," said Sadiq with a smile.

The class erupted in cheers.

"Settle down, everyone," said Ms Battersby. "We have one more candidate. Abdirahman Nur. Come on up, Manny!"

Manny walked to the front of the class and took a deep breath.

"Hi, everyone," Manny started. "I was going to run for president. But I've changed my mind. I've decided to run as Sadiq's vice president!"

"What?" Sadiq whispered to Zaza.

"Wait, let's see what he has to say," said Zaza.

"Sadiq has a lot of good ideas!" Manny went on. "I didn't really come up with any ideas. I will be voting for Sadiq for president. I hope you all will too!"

"What?" Sadiq said to Zaza, louder this time. "Did he say he would vote for me?"

"I think he did!" said Zaza, laughing.

The whole class was talking at the same time. Some students were clapping for Manny and Sadiq. Some kids gave Manny fist bumps as he walked back to his desk.

After speeches for the other positions, Ms Battersby handed out voting cards. The cards had a line for each of the four positions.

```
PRESIDENT_____
VICE PRESIDENT _____
SECRETARY_____
TREASURER_____
```

Everyone wrote down their vote and put it in a box on Ms Battersby's desk. Soon, all the votes had been cast.

"Okay, everyone," said Ms Battersby. "I will count the votes during break time."

Break seemed to last forever. Sadiq didn't even join the kids playing football. He couldn't focus on that today! He was too excited about the election.

"I wonder how everyone will vote," said Zaza. "I am so excited for you!"

At last, it was time to go back to the classroom. Ms Battersby announced the results once everyone sat down.

"The position of secretary goes to Owen. Our treasurer will be Suliat. Manny has been elected as vice president. And our new class president is Sadiq!" she said. "Congratulations to you all!"

"Yay!" shouted Zaza. "Congrats, Sadiq! Well done, Manny!"

"Congrats, Manny!" said Sadiq, shaking his friend's hand. "Thank you for your support. I am so glad you're my vice president. We can make a lot of good changes together."

"Thank you, Sadiq!" said Manny. "You really did have a lot of good ideas. I am sorry I was upset before. Friends again?"

"Friends forever!" said Sadiq, laughing and hugging his friend.

He couldn't wait to begin his job as class president!

GLOSSARY

budget a plan for how money will be earned and spent

campaign the steps taken by a candidate to try to win an election

candidate a person who is running for a position in an election

cheque a piece of paper that allows you to give money to someone else through a bank

election a process where people vote for who they want in office

government a system that is used to run a country and make rules

president a person who is elected by the people in a country or other community to lead them

samosa fried pastry filled with spicy beef, chicken, fish or vegetables

secretary a person who helps a group take notes and keep records about the group's plans and decisions

treasurer a person who manages money for a group

vice president a person who helps a president with their work or duties

TALK ABOUT IT

1. Ms Battersby said that doing hard things is how we grow. What do you think she meant by that?

2. What were Sadiq's reasons for running for president? Why do you think they were so important to him?

3. Running for president is hard for Sadiq. Who supported him along the way? How did each of these people help him?

WRITE IT DOWN

1. Imagine you are running for president of your class. What ideas do you have to help people? Write the speech you would give.

2. Have you ever had to compete against a friend? How did it feel? Write about what happened.

3. Write a story for Sadiq's school newspaper about the election. You can interview Sadiq, Manny and others for your story.

MAKE A CAMPAIGN POSTER

Sadiq and Manny made posters in their campaigns for class president. Make your own campaign poster. Imagine you are running for class president. Your poster explains why people should vote for you.

WHAT YOU NEED:

- plain paper
- pencil
- coloured felt-tips
- card

WHAT TO DO:

1. Come up with a headline for your poster. It could be "[Your Name] for Prez!" or "Vote 4 [Your Name]." Or it could be something more creative, like a rhyming phrase, pun or joke using your name.

2. Brainstorm 2–4 ideas for what you will do if elected. How will you make things better for your classmates?

3. Do you want your poster to include art? Consider drawing stars, flowers, a voting card or something else.

4. Choose a design from the examples below, or make up your own.

5. Practise drawing your design with pencil on the plain paper. Make another practice poster if you want to keep improving it.

6. When you like the way your practice poster looks, repeat the design on your card using the coloured felt-tips.

CREATORS

Siman Nuurali grew up in Kenya. She now lives in Minnesota, USA. Siman and her family are Somali – just like Sadiq and his family! She and her five children love to play badminton and board games together. Siman works at the Children's Hospital and in her free time she enjoys writing and reading.

Christos Skaltsas was born and raised in Athens, Greece. For the past fifteen years, he has worked as a freelance illustrator for children's book publishers. In his free time, he loves playing with his son, collecting vinyl records and travelling around the world.